Mama,
If You Had a Wish

Mama,
If You Had a Wish

By Jeanne Modesitt
Illustrated by Robin Spowart

GREEN TIGER PRESS
Published by Simon & Schuster
New York London Toronto Sydney Tokyo Singapore

GREEN TIGER PRESS
Simon & Schuster Building, Rockefeller Center
1230 Avenue of the Americas, New York, New York 10020
Text copyright © 1993 by Jeanne Modesitt
Illustrations copyright © 1993 by Robin Spowart
GREEN TIGER PRESS is an imprint of Simon & Schuster.
Designed by Alan Benjamin.
Manufactured in the United States of America

10 9 8 7 6 5 4 3

Library of Congress Cataloging-in-Publication Data
Modesitt, Jeanne, Mama, if you had a wish / by Jeanne Modesitt ;
illustrated by Robin Spowart. p. cm. Summary: If Little Bunny's
mother could have one wish about her child,
it would be to keep Little Bunny unchanged and loved by her.
[1. Mother and child—Fiction. 2. Individuality—Fiction,
3. Rabbits—Fiction. 4. Wishes—Fiction.]
I. Spowart, Robin, ill. II. Title. PZ7.M715Mam 1993
[E]—dc20 91-31354 CIP ISBN: 0-671-75437-8

To all of us.

"Mama," asked Little Bunny, "if you had a wish,

would you wish I never cried?"

"No, Little Bunny," answered Mama, "but it does make me sad to see you cry."

"Would you wish I was
   brave all the time, and never
   got scared of anything?"

"No, Little Bunny," said Mama.
"We all get scared sometimes."

"What about when I get mad at you?"
 asked Little Bunny.
"Would you wish I never did that?"

"No, Little Bunny," said Mama.
"I love you when you are mad at me,
and I love you when you are not."

"I bet I know what you would wish," said Little Bunny. "You would wish I never made any mistakes."

"No, Little Bunny," said Mama,
"I love you no matter how many
mistakes you make."

"Even big giant mistakes?"
"Even big giant mistakes."

"Well," said Little Bunny,
"you probably would wish I looked
different, wouldn't you?"

"No, Little Bunny," said Mama.
"I wouldn't wish you to look
any different than you do."

Little Bunny was quiet for a moment. "Mama, if you could make one wish about me, what would it be?"

"I would wish for you to be yourself," said Mama, "because I love you just the way you are."